Bronco Charlie
and the
Pony Express

BY MARLENE TARG BRILL
ILLUSTRATIONS BY CRAIG ORBACK

M Millbrook Press/Minneapolis

The author wishes to thank Jacqueline Lewin, Curator of History at the Pony Express Museum, for telling her about Bronco Charlie and Lois Miller Ellsworth, Charlie's great-grandniece, for setting the record straight about his tall tales.

Dialogue in this book came from Bronco Charlie's own stories collected by Gladys Shaw Erskine in *Broncho Charlie: Saga of the Saddle* (New York: Thomas Y. Crowell Co., 1934) and Lois Miller Ellsworth in *Tales of Broncho Charlie* (Santa Cruz, CA: Hollis Books, 1999).

The illustrator would like to thank the models who were used for the oil paintings, most especially Collin Foote as Bronco Charlie, as well as Gary and Eileen Orback, who represent assorted characters. Thanks also to Jessica Silks for modeling and for her help with photography.

Charlie spelled his name *Broncho* Charlie. We have chosen to use the modern spelling of his name in this book.

This book is available in two editions:
Library binding by Millbrook Press
  A division of Lerner Publishing Group, Inc.
Soft cover by First Avenue Editions
  An imprint of Lerner Publishing Group, Inc.
241 First Avenue North
Minneapolis, MN 55401 USA

For reading levels and more information, look up this title at www.lernerbooks.com.

Library of Congress Cataloging-in-Publication Data

Brill, Marlene Targ.
    Bronco Charlie and the Pony Express / by Marlene Targ Brill ; illustrations by Craig Orback.
      p.   cm. — (On my own history)
    Summary: Relates how, in 1861, a boy named Charlie Miller became the youngest rider for the Pony Express, a mail service that linked the East and West Coasts of the United States.
    ISBN 978–1–57505–587–9 (lib. bdg. : alk. paper)
    ISBN 978–1–57505–618–0 (pbk. : alk. paper)
    ISBN 978–1–57505–773–6 (EB pdf)
    1. Pony express—History—Juvenile literature. 2. Miller, Charlie, b. 1850—Juvenile literature. 3. Postal service—United States—History—Juvenile literature. [1. Pony express. 2. Miller, Charlie, b. 1850. 3. Postal service—History.] I. Orback, Craig, ill. II. Title. III. Series.
HE6375.P65 B75 2004
383'.143'092—dc21   2002153946

Manufactured in the United States of America
7-42493-7501-7/6/2016

To girls and boys who love adventure, like
Charlie. Follow your dreams. —M. T. B.

For my dad Gary who, like Charlie, made
his own journey to California —C. S. O.

Sacramento Valley,
California, 1860

Julius jumped onto his first
bucking bronco.
The wild horse leaped to the left.
It whirled to the right.
It tried hard to shake
the 10-year-old boy loose.

But Julius clung to the reins
until his fingers burned.
Then the animal tripped.
Julius tumbled to the ground.
Tears filled his eyes.

Julius Miller loved horses.

More than anything, he wanted to prove he
could be a cowboy.

When he was nine years old,
his father sent him to sea
to become a sailor.

But Julius hated the sea.

He jumped ship in California.

There he met a cowboy named Juan
who worked at a cattle ranch.

Juan took Julius back to the ranch with him.

Juan was the best horse tamer there.

He taught Julius to ride horses,
rope cows, and hunt bears.

He was teaching Julius
how to tame a wild horse.

If Julius could tame this one,
the animal would be his.

Julius forced back his tears
at the sound of cowboys laughing.
They thought Julius was too small
to tame such a big, wild horse.
But he showed them.
Julius got back on the bronco
and stayed on.
After that, the men called him
Bronco Charlie.
The name stuck.

Bronco Charlie tamed that first horse
and many others.
After a year, he started itching
for a new adventure.
One night, a scruffy, old cowboy
drifted into camp.
He dazzled Charlie with stories
about the new Pony Express.
Pony Express riders
changed how people got news.
No railroads or good roads ran between
Missouri and California in 1861.
So California's scattered towns were
cut off from the rest of the country.

Express riders traveled through desert,
rocky mountains, and Indian country.
They rode all night, changing horses
at stations 15 miles apart.
They took an oath to stay on time.

Express riders carried mail across
2,000 miles in just 10 days.
That was 20 days faster than stagecoaches
and 100 days quicker than boats!
The old cowboy said that the Express used
riders a little older than Charlie.
Charlie dreamed of being
part of the Pony Express.
Next chance he had,
he hightailed it from the ranch.
He wanted to see the
Pony Express for himself.

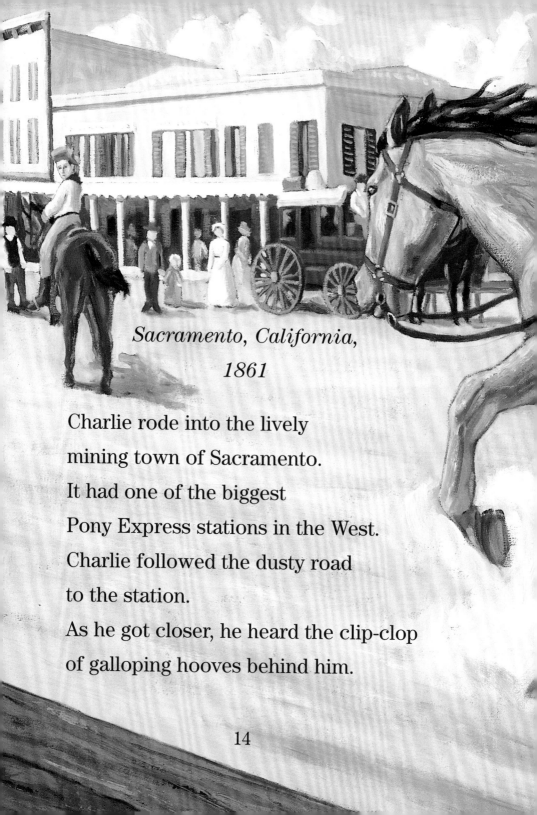

Sacramento, California,
1861

Charlie rode into the lively
mining town of Sacramento.
It had one of the biggest
Pony Express stations in the West.
Charlie followed the dusty road
to the station.
As he got closer, he heard the clip-clop
of galloping hooves behind him.

His heart pounded.

Was he about to see

a Pony Express rider?

Charlie turned.

All he saw was a horse with a mailbag

and an empty saddle.

People flooded into the street
to see the riderless horse.
It was a Pony Express horse for sure.
But no one knew what had happened
to the rider.
"What you going to do now?"
a woman asked the stationmaster.
"The mail will be late this time,"
he answered.
"We'll have to wait for the next rider."

Everyone grew quiet.

Charlie looked at their worried faces.

He saw fear for the missing rider.

But he also saw hunger for news

from back East.

Folks in the next town

would hunger for it too.

That spring, war had broken out between

states in the North and the South.

Most Californians had family

in those states.

Charlie pushed to the front of the crowd.

"I can ride," he said.

All eyes turned toward him.

Everyone grew quiet.

Charlie looked at their worried faces.

He saw fear for the missing rider.

But he also saw hunger for news

from back East.

Folks in the next town

would hunger for it too.

That spring, war had broken out between

states in the North and the South.

Most Californians had family

in those states.

Charlie pushed to the front of the crowd.

"I can ride," he said.

All eyes turned toward him.

Some men said that Charlie
looked too young.
Pony Express riders handled fast,
headstrong horses.
Riders faced bears, wolves,
and rattlesnakes.
And they had to steer clear
of unfriendly Indians.

White settlers had been taking away
Indian land for many years.
Some Indians fought back
by attacking travelers.
"If you'll give me a fightin' chance, I'll show
you what I can do," Charlie said.

Before anyone could answer,
Charlie handed his horse to a stranger.
Then he swung into the saddle
of the waiting Pony Express horse.
The stationmaster looked around.
What choice did he have?
He gave Charlie a horn.

He said the next station was in Placerville,
about 50 miles away.
Charlie was to blow the horn
when he neared the station.
The sound would tell the men there to get a
fresh horse ready for another rider.
Then the stationmaster shook Charlie's
hand and slapped the horse's backside.

Charlie was off!
He followed a dirt road
until he reached the mountains.
Soon the town disappeared.
A wide grin spread over Charlie's face.
For this one day,
he was a true Pony Express rider.

Charlie felt so important
he thought his buttons would pop.
But he knew the ride wouldn't be easy.
There were no roads or markings
to help him find the way to Placerville.
He was on a horse he'd never ridden.
And he had to travel up and down
steep mountain passes.

Already the horse slipped
climbing the rocky slopes.
Charlie patted the horse to steady him.
As they came around a bend,
the wind picked up.
Raindrops dotted Charlie's face.
Before long, sheets of blinding rain
soaked his clothes.
Charlie reached for the soft leather
mail pouch.
Oiled silk sealed its pockets.
He knew the letters inside
would stay dry.

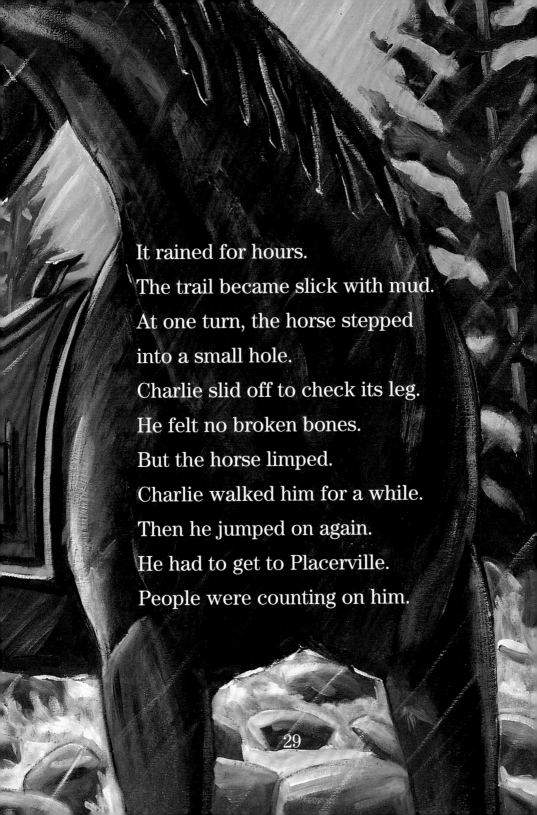

It rained for hours.

The trail became slick with mud.

At one turn, the horse stepped

into a small hole.

Charlie slid off to check its leg.

He felt no broken bones.

But the horse limped.

Charlie walked him for a while.

Then he jumped on again.

He had to get to Placerville.

People were counting on him.

As they rounded another bend,
the rain stopped.
The late afternoon sun appeared.
For a while, a yellow glow
lit the mountainside.
Then blackness closed around them.
Charlie shivered.
He pulled his damp shirt tighter.

He had never been in the mountains
by himself at night.
He always had cowboys singing
or a herd of cattle to keep him company.
Every critter cry and breaking twig
seemed louder in the darkness.
Charlie remembered the rider
whose place he had taken.
What could have happened to him? Indians?
Wolves? A bad fall?

As the clouds cleared,

the moon came out.

At first, Charlie welcomed the light.

Then moon shadows

began to play tricks on him.

Animals and birds looked like monsters.

Tree branches seemed like grabbing arms.

Suddenly, the horse leaped up in terror and

spun around.

Charlie tried to calm the spooked animal.

But out of the corner of his eye,

he saw someone hiding in the trees.

The man raised a huge club.

Was he an Indian?

Charlie held his breath.
He slowly pulled a knife
from his belt.
He was about to throw it
when the wind kicked up.
The man moved.
Charlie burst out laughing.
The man was really branches
and leaves.
For now, Charlie was safe.

After many hours more,
the sun came up.
Charlie stopped on a ridge
overlooking a small town.
It was Placerville!
A Pony Express sign hung
on the last cabin on the road.
He rode down the only mud road
into the center of town.

Then he reached for his horn
and blew hard.
The stationmaster raced from the cabin
to saddle a fresh horse.
People rushed out of doorways
to hear the latest news.

The stationmaster pulled the letters
for Placerville from Charlie's mailbag.
Then he stuffed other mail into the bag
and sealed it again.
A new rider grabbed the bag
and jumped onto the fresh horse.
The stationmaster turned to Charlie.
He had never seen such a young
Pony Express rider.
He asked Charlie how he came to ride.
Charlie explained as best he could.
But he was too tired to talk much.
The man showed him a bed
where he could sleep.
He said a stagecoach would take him
back to Sacramento the next night.
Charlie wished he could ride
for the Pony Express instead.

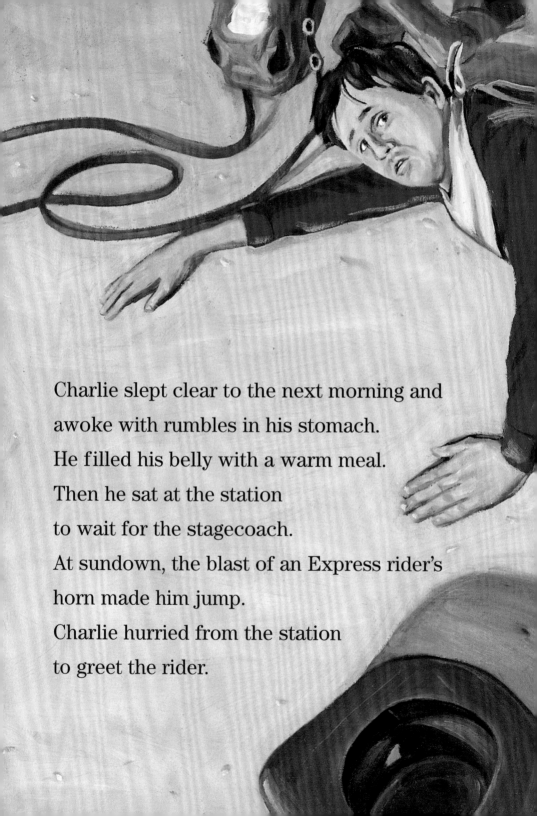

Charlie slept clear to the next morning and
awoke with rumbles in his stomach.
He filled his belly with a warm meal.
Then he sat at the station
to wait for the stagecoach.
At sundown, the blast of an Express rider's
horn made him jump.
Charlie hurried from the station
to greet the rider.

But something was wrong.
The rider bumped from side to side,
trying to stay in the saddle.
Then he toppled off his horse
and sagged to the ground.
He said Indians had shot him
about 10 miles back.

Charlie knew the man
couldn't deliver the mail.
So Charlie picked up the mailbag.
He climbed on a fresh horse.
And he pointed it toward Sacramento.
No one tried to stop him.
The stationmaster knew he could ride
as fast as any Pony Express man.

This time, the trip went smoother.
Charlie remembered the way back.
He knew the sounds
of mountain animals and birds.
He laughed at moonlit shadows
from trees and rocks.
He felt like he'd been delivering mail
for years.

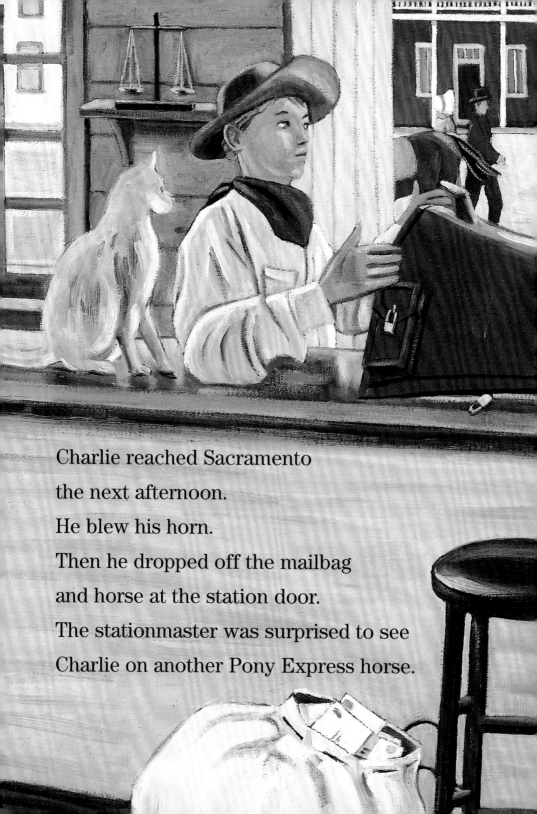

Charlie reached Sacramento
the next afternoon.
He blew his horn.
Then he dropped off the mailbag
and horse at the station door.
The stationmaster was surprised to see
Charlie on another Pony Express horse.

Charlie hoped the man would hire him
on the spot.
But he only said that Charlie
could rest in the office.
Then he would have to go home.

The next morning,

voices woke Charlie.

The men at the station had been talking.

They said Charlie proved himself.

He was good enough

to ride the Pony Express.

Did he want the job?

Charlie wanted it more than anything!

Charlie was sworn in at the station

that day.

Charlie gave his word he would never

fight, drink, or curse.

And the youngest Pony Express rider

promised to always deliver

the mail on time.

Afterword

Charlie delivered mail for another five months. On October 18, 1861, the first telegraph message was sent. Telegraph messages traveled across the country through wires. Each message arrived in a flash. Eight days later, the Pony Express closed.

Charlie continued to find adventures riding horses. He traveled the world with Buffalo Bill's Wild West Show. He tamed horses for Teddy Roosevelt, who later became a U.S. president. He protected U.S. borders as a Texas Ranger. Yet he always treasured his days as a Pony Express rider.

In 1931, Bronco Charlie made one last ride to deliver mail. By then, cars had replaced horses. Some people flew by airplane. Still, Charlie wanted to travel from New York City to San Francisco by horseback. He rode 30 miles a day through snow, rain, and sandstorms. The trip took seven months and 23 days. At age 81, Charlie was the only person ever to cross the country on a horse.

Bronco Charlie liked to thrill listeners with stories of the Pony Express and his last mail run. He knew how to spin a good tale. Sometimes he changed the facts from one telling to the next. In 1934, many of his stories went into a book.

Bronco Charlie died at age 105, the longest living Pony Express rider. Years later, his great-grandniece discovered the true story of how he became the youngest rider on the Pony Express. That story lives on.